THE INFAMOUS RATSOS

Are Tough, Tough, Tough!

3 Books in 1

Kara LaReau

illustrated by Matt Myers

CANDLEWICK PRESS

The Infamous Ratsos
Library of Congress Catalog Card Number 2016938103
ISBN 978-0-7636-7636-0 (hardcover)
ISBN 978-0-7636-9875-1 (paperback)

The Infamous Ratsos Are Not Afraid
Library of Congress Catalog Card Number 2017953740
ISBN 978-0-7636-7637-7 (hardcover)
ISBN 978-1-5362-0368-4 (paperback)

The Infamous Ratsos: Project Fluffy
Library of Congress Catalog Card Number 2018959922
ISBN 978-1-5362-0005-8 (hardcover)
ISBN 978-1-5362-0880-1 (paperback)

ISBN 978-1-5362-2299-9 (trade paperback collection)

21 22 23 24 25 26 TRC 10 9 8 7 6 5 4 3 2 1

Printed in Eagan, MN, USA

This book was typeset in Scala.
The illustrations were done in ink and watercolor.

Candlewick Press
99 Dover Street
Somerville, Massachusetts 02144

www.candlewick.com

- CONTENTS -

- BOOK ONE -

THE INFAMOUS RATSOS

For my grandfather,
the original Ralphie xo
K. L.

For Bruce,
my childhood coconspirator
in nefarious deeds
M. M.

HANG TOUGH

This is Louie Ratso. This is Ralphie Ratso.

The Ratso brothers live in the Big City. They live in this apartment with their father, Big Lou.

"There are two kinds of people in this world," Big Lou likes to say. "Those who are tough, and those who are soft."

Big Lou is tough, tough, tough. He drives a truck and a forklift and sometimes a snowplow. He hardly ever smiles.

As for the Ratso brothers' mother, she's been gone for a little while now, which is very sad. The Ratso brothers don't like to think about Mama Ratso. Big Lou doesn't like to think about Mama Ratso either.

"Hang tough," he grumbles each morning as he leaves for work, slamming the door behind him.

- 2 -
HATS OFF

After Big Lou leaves for work each morning, the Ratso brothers go to school. Louie is in the fifth grade and Ralphie is in third. They walk to school, because walking is tough. Taking the bus is for softies.

The Ratso brothers don't talk very much on their way to school. Talking a lot is also for softies. Their father hardly ever talks at all. Big Lou is a man of action, not words.

"Let's do something," Louie says to Ralphie. "Something to make us *look* tough."

"Like what?" Ralphie asks.

"Leave the thinking to me," says Louie. He considers himself the smart one.

At recess, Louie and Ralphie meet on the playground. They lean against the wall and glare at everyone and take turns spitting on the blacktop. Leaning and glaring and spitting are tough. Running and playing are for softies.

Chad Badgerton is wearing a new hat today. It is red, and it is too small for his head.

Louie has an idea.

"We'd look tough if we took Chad's hat," he suggests.

"Chad is bigger than we are," Ralphie reminds him. "A *lot* bigger."

"Well, there are two of us, and only one of him," Louie says.

"Righto," Ralphie says. He gives his brother a nod.

Ralphie distracts Chad while Louie jumps up and swipes the hat from his head.

"Hey!" cries Chad. "You can't do that!"

"We just did," shout the Ratso brothers. "Nyah-nyah!"

"I think I feel tougher," says Ralphie.

"My head is about to feel warmer, that's for sure," says Louie. But before he can put on the hat, Tiny Crawley comes running over, along with Miss Beavers, the third-grade teacher.

"You rescued my hat!" Tiny exclaims. He takes it from Louie.

"*Your* hat?" say the Ratso brothers.

"Chad took it from me on the bus," Tiny says. "He's a big bully."

"That was nice of you boys, sticking up for Tiny," says Miss Beavers.

"We're not nice, we're TOUGH," Louie tries to explain.

"Nyah-nyah!" Ralphie repeats.

But no one is listening. Instead, everyone on the playground is looking at the Ratso brothers like they're heroes. Everyone except for Chad Badgerton, who is on his way to the principal's office.

"I wish *we* were going to the principal's office," Ralphie says.

"We need to step up our game," decides Louie.

3

THE SNOW JOB

When the Ratso brothers wake up, it's snowing. Everything in the Big City looks like it's draped in white sheets.

"No school today, boys," says Big Lou. "The buses can't get down the roads."

"Buses are for softies," says Louie.

"I'm off to do some snowplowing," grumbles Big Lou. "Hang tough. And try not to get into too much trouble while I'm gone." He slams the door behind him.

"I have an idea," says Louie.

"How much trouble will it get us into?" asks Ralphie.

"Plenty," says Louie. "Let's go."

The Ratso brothers put on their snow pants and coats and gloves and boots and scarves and hats. They grab their shovels and go outside. It is still snowing.

"I can't see," says Ralphie. "What's the plan?"

"The plan is that we shovel all the snow from the sidewalk and pile it all up in front of Mr. O'Hare's store. When he comes down for work this morning, he won't be able to open the door!"

"That's mean," says Ralphie.

"That's *tough*," says Louie.

"Righto," Ralphie says, cracking his knuckles. "Let's make some trouble."

The Ratso brothers go out to the side-walk and begin shoveling. They shovel and shovel and shovel, even when the snow starts falling so heavily they can't see a thing.

"This is hard work," says Ralphie.

"It will make us tougher," says Louie. "Keep shoveling."

"This way," says Ralphie.

"No, this way," says Louie.

"I'm pretty sure it's this way," says Ralphie.

"I'm pretty sure I'm the big brother," says Louie. "*This* way."

The brothers shovel and shovel until they can't shovel anymore. They fall back onto a snowdrift.

"I'm tired," Ralphie says with a yawn.

"Me, too," admits Louie. Soon the Ratso brothers are asleep.

"Why, you boys are as good as gold!" a voice exclaims.

"What?" says Louie. He nudges Ralphie awake.

Mr. O'Hare is in the doorway of his store, tears forming in his eyes. "It would have taken me all day to shovel that. I'm going to tell every one of my customers how thoughtful you are!"

"We're not thoughtful, we're TOUGH!" insists Louie. But Mr. O'Hare isn't listening; he's already open for business, with a little extra spring in his step.

"How did he get out?" asks Ralphie.

"We ended up shoveling all the snow away from Mr. O'Hare's door instead of *toward* it," Louie explains. "Somehow, we got turned around."

"Somehow?" says Ralphie.

"Don't worry," says Louie. "I'm sure another idea will come to me."

"Sure, *big brother,*" says Ralphie.

The Ratso brothers trudge home.

They spend the day shivering in front of the heater in their long johns, drinking hot chocolate.

4

THE FLUFFY SPECIAL

This is **Florinda Rabbitski.** She's just moved to the Big City," Mr. Ferretti announces to his students, including Louie.

"I like being called Fluffy," Florinda says meekly, looking at the floor.

"Her name sounds funny. And she looks weird," says Chad Badgerton.

At lunch, no one sits with Fluffy Rabbitski. She picks at her lunch of lettuce and raw vegetables and carrot juice. She seems sad, and lonely.

As always, the Ratso brothers sit together and eat their cheddar cheese sandwiches.

"Check out the new girl," says Louie.

"She smells like carrots," says Ralphie.

"Her name is Fluffy Rabbitski. She seems like a softie," says Louie. "Even her name sounds soft." He wrinkles his nose. And then he reaches into his brain and picks out another tough idea.

That night, before they go to bed, the Ratso brothers make their cheddar cheese sandwiches for the next day.

They also make a very special
sandwich, piled high with the worst
foods they can find in the refrigerator.

"Fluffy Rabbitski is in for a big,
stinky surprise," Louie says.

At lunch the next day, Fluffy
Rabbitski is about to sit by herself

again when Ralphie gives her a whistle. Louie pats the seat next to him.

"Why don't you eat with us?" he suggests.

"Thank you," says Fluffy. She sits down and quietly takes out her sad little lunch of lettuce and raw vegetables and carrot juice.

"We thought you might like a real Big City treat," Louie says, pushing the sandwich in front of her. "We call it the Fluffy Special. We made it just for you."

Fluffy unwraps the sandwich and takes a sniff. Her eyes grow wide. Ralphie doesn't know whether to laugh or pinch his nose. The sandwich smells beyond awful.

But then Fluffy Rabbitski grabs the sandwich with both paws and takes a huge bite.

"Mmmmm," she says, swallowing. "Pickled mushrooms and beets and eggplant, just like my nana used to make! How did you know?"

"We didn't," Louie says. But Fluffy is too busy enjoying her sandwich to care. When she finishes, she pats her belly and looks at the Ratso brothers with shining eyes.

"I've been missing my old house and my nana since we moved here," she explains. "You two are the first to make me feel at home. I can't wait to tell everyone how generous you've been to me."

"We're not generous. We're TOUGH!" Louie insists. But Fluffy Rabbitski is not listening. She's licking her lips, still tasting that sandwich.

"Is this seat taken?" asks Tiny Crawley, sliding in next to Fluffy.

Louie throws up his hands.

"Maybe *I* should come up with the next idea," suggests Ralphie.

5

THE PORCUPINI WINDOW

On the way home from school on Friday, the Ratso brothers pass by Mrs. Porcupini's house. Mrs. Porcupini spends her days leaning against her cane and staring out her window with a sour expression on her face,

like she's just sucked on a pickle. She
seems to reserve her sourest looks for
the Ratso brothers.

Ralphie Ratso's brain is not quite as big as his brother's, but it is filled to the brim with ideas. He reaches in and pulls out a nasty one.

After Big Lou gets home and the Ratso brothers eat their dinner and wash the dishes and put them away and get into bed and turn out the light, Ralphie whispers his plan to his brother.

Then he says, "After tonight, everyone in the neighborhood will know how tough the Ratso brothers are."

They wait until they hear Big Lou's snoring, and then they sneak out of the apartment and down the stairs and outside. They creep over to Mrs. Porcupini's house. Ralphie reaches into his pockets and pulls out two big bars of soap.

"Let's teach that prickly pickle not to give us sour looks," he whispers. "When she looks out her window tomorrow morning, she won't be able to see a thing!"

"Pretty clever," says Louie. Though he still considers himself the smart one.

The brothers begin rubbing soap all over Mrs. Porcupini's window. When they're done, they have plenty of soap left over.

"Let's keep going," says Ralphie.

The Ratso brothers soap each and every one of Mrs. Porcupini's windows. By the time they're done, the sun is coming up. Louie lets out a big, long yawn.

"Shhh!" says Ralphie.

But the sound has already woken up Mrs. Porcupini. She goes to the picture window and lets out a little yelp of surprise.

The Ratso brothers start running. But they've been awake all night soaping windows, so they're too tired to run very fast. And Mrs. Porcupini is already calling for them from her front porch, so they don't get very far.

"Louie and Ralphie Ratso!" she shouts. "Come here this *instant!*"

"We're really in trouble now," Ralphie says.

"Finally," says Louie.

When they climb the steps of the front porch, the Ratso brothers can

see that Mrs. Porcupini's sour-pickle expression is gone. In its place is an expression that looks very much like delight.

"I haven't been able to wash my own windows since I hurt my knee," Mrs. Porcupini explains. "It pains me to look out a dirty window. You boys saw someone in need and did something about it. I can't wait to tell everyone in the neighborhood how helpful you two are!"

"We're not helpful, we're TOUGH!" Ralphie insists.

But Mrs. Porcupini isn't listening; she is too busy showing them where the garden hose is and how to hook it up. The Ratso brothers spend the rest of the morning rinsing off all the soap until Mrs. Porcupini's windows sparkle in the sun.

6

"HE DID IT"

When they get home, the Ratso brothers want nothing more than to climb into bed and sleep all day. But that isn't going to happen. Because waiting for them in the kitchen is their father. In his hand is an open letter, printed on crisp white paper.

"This just came from the school," Big Lou says. "Do you boys have something you'd like to tell me?"

"He did it," the Ratso brothers say at the same time, each pointing at the other.

"You've both been busy. According to Mr. Ferretti, you welcomed a new student to the school and made her lunch. And according to Miss Beavers, you stopped a bully from terrorizing another student," Big Lou says, rereading the letter. "And then, this morning, when I went out to get the mail, Mr. O'Hare told me you two shoveled his sidewalk during the snowstorm."

"It was an accident," Ralphie tries to explain.

"Which part?" asks Big Lou.

"All of it," says Louie.

"So you're not really nice, or kind, or thoughtful, like everyone's saying?" Big Lou asks.

"No, and we're not helpful either, so don't listen to whatever Mrs. Porcupini tells you," Ralphie says. "We're TOUGH!"

"We just want to be like you," admits Louie.

"Like me?" says Big Lou.

"Yeah, you're tough. Being nice and helpful is for softies," says Ralphie.

Big Lou looks at the photo of Mama Ratso on the wall. He hangs his head.

"The last thing you want is to be like me," he says. "It's been hard on all of us since your mother's been gone. But you two have found a way to take care of yourselves and be good to others. *I* should be trying to be more like *you.*"

Louie and Ralphie blink.

They look at the photo of Mama, too. They think about how soft and warm she was. And how good she was to them.

"Being tough all the time is so . . . so . . . *tough*," says their father. He puts his arms around the Ratso brothers and pulls them close.

"I think I have something in my eye," says Louie.

"Me, too," says Ralphie.

Before long, they are crying, Big Lou loudest of all.

- 7 -

TOUGH
ENOUGH

This is Louie Ratso. This is Ralphie
Ratso. This is Big Lou Ratso.

Everyone in the Big City knows
the Ratsos. And everyone stays out of
their way. Because who knows what
they might be up to next?

They might just rake and bag your
leaves for you on a windy day.

You might wake up one morning to see they've fixed your broken fence.

They might even push you on the playground swing.

"Life is tough enough," says Big Lou. "We might as well try to make it easier for one another, whenever we can."

"No worries. I've got big plans for us,"
says Louie. He still considers himself
the smart one. So does Fluffy Rabbitski.

"Whatever your plans are, count me
in!" says Fluffy.

"Whee!" says Tiny Crawley. "This is fun!"

"Righto!" says Ralphie.

BOOK TWO

Are Not Afraid

For Catherine
K. L.

For Pat, who can find treasure
in any junk pile
M. M.

JUNK, JUNK, EVERYWHERE

This is Louie Ratso. This is Ralphie Ratso.

The Ratso brothers are walking home from the Big City Carnival.

"I love the carnival," Ralphie says. He takes an extra-big bite of his cotton candy.

"Me, too," says Louie. "I love the rides and the food and the games in the arcade."

"The arcade games are my favorite," Ralphie says. "I love the ringtoss and the whack-a-mole and the rope climb and the fortune-teller and the high striker. And the prizes."

"There's only one thing I don't love about the carnival," Louie says. "The

fact that it only happens once a year. I wish we could go there every day."

When the Ratsos reach their neighborhood, they walk extra fast as they pass the Haunted House. That's what all the kids in the neighborhood call the run-down house on the corner. They say a ghost lives there who only comes out at night.

Louie always gets goose bumps when he walks past the Haunted House. He doesn't tell Ralphie this. Louie is the older brother, so he is supposed to be the braver one.

"Whoa . . . that's a lot of junk," Ralphie says. He points to the lot next to the Haunted House. Louie has never really noticed the lot because he's too busy trying to hide his goose bumps. But if there is one thing the Ratsos love, it's junk, especially someone else's old junk. And this lot is full of it.

Before the Ratsos know it, they are rummaging through the junk piles. And before Louie Ratso knows it, his brain is working on something.

"I know that look," Ralphie says. "You have an idea."

"Yep. A big one," says Louie.

"Um . . . does it involve cleaning?" Ralphie asks. Cleaning is Ralphie's least-favorite activity.

"It does," says Louie. "But it's going to be fun. Trust me."

Ralphie considers the mess all around them. "Where do we start?"

"First, we'll need help," Louie says.

"A lot of it."

- 2 -
FUN TIME

When we're done cleaning, I think we should build a clubhouse," suggests Tiny Crawley.

"I think we should plant a garden," says Fluffy Rabbitski. "With lettuce and carrots and cucumbers."

"We should bring a bunch of tents and sleeping bags here and camp out. We can make s'mores!" says Chad Badgerton.

"All of those are good ideas," says Louie Ratso. "But I have a *great* idea. We're going to turn this into . . . the Big City FunTime Arcade!"

"What's an arcade?" Fluffy asks.

"It's where you play video games," Tiny explains. "Are we going to play video games here?"

"Not video games," Louie explains. "This arcade will have *carnival* games."

"Like the arcade at the Big City Carnival?" Ralphie asks.

"Yep. But the Big City Carnival only comes around once a year," Louie reminds them. "The Big City FunTime Arcade will be around all year long!"

"How are we going to turn *this* into an arcade?" Chad asks.

"I have it all planned out," Louie says. "We'll make the games using some of this junk, and we'll clear out the rest. We'll have an entrance, where we'll sell tickets."

"And we have to have prizes. Lots

of prizes," Ralphie says.

"I figure we can give away our old toys," Louie says. "When we make enough money from the tickets, we can buy better stuff."

"I have lots of old toys at home," says Tiny.

"Me, too," says Fluffy.

"Excellent. OK, back to work, team!" shouts Louie. "First we clean. Then we build. Then we *play*!"

"What about all the old furniture over there?" Chad says. He points to the pile of junk closest to the Haunted

House. Just looking in the direction of the house gives Louie a wave of goose bumps. He pretends to consult his plans extra carefully.

"You take care of it, Chad," Louie says.

"Why don't *you* take care of it?" Chad asks.

"I'm *supervising*," Louie says.

"I thought we were supposed to be a team," Chad says. "Or maybe you're *afraid* to go over there?"

"I'm not afraid," says Louie. "I just have a lot of work to oversee."

Chad's stomach growls. "We'd better
be done soon. It's almost dinnertime,"
he says. The Ratsos used to think Chad
was mean, until they realized he gets

cranky when he's hungry, which is almost all the time.

"Never fear," says Ralphie. "I brought emergency snacks for Chad."

As Chad eats and cleans, Louie glances up at the house. He swears he sees something white move behind one of the boarded-up windows. Louie shivers. Did he just see . . . a ghost?

3

RALPHIE LOVES STINKY

The next day is a Monday. The Ratsos hate Mondays. Ralphie hates this Monday in particular, because he has a spelling test.

In the middle of the test, Ralphie hears something roll under his chair.

It's a purple pen. The purple pen belongs to Stinky Stanko, the girl who sits behind him. Ralphie picks it up and hands it to her, but he makes sure not to touch her. Everyone knows Stinky Stanko stinks.

"Thank you," says Stinky.

"You're welcome," mumbles Ralphie. He goes back to trying to spell the word *trepidation*.

By lunchtime, Ralphie is pretty sure this is the worst Monday ever. Everyone in the lunchroom seems to be singing the same song. The song happens to be about him.

"Ralphie and Stinky up in a tree, K-I-S-S-I-N-G!"

"Is it true?" Tiny asks him. "Do you really have a thing for Stinky Stanko?"

Ralphie pinches his nose. "P.U.," he says.

"Who is Stinky Stanko?" asks Fluffy.

"Her," Louie says. He points out Stinky, sitting at a table by herself. "She's in Ralphie's class. Everyone knows she smells bad, so no one will go near her."

"Is her name really *Stinky?*" asks Fluffy.

"That's just her nickname— though I don't even know what her real name is," says Tiny.

"Ralphie loves Stinky! Ralphie loves Stinky!" chants Kurt Musky.

"I do not! She STINKS!" shouts Ralphie.

"If you don't like her, why does everyone think you do?" asks Tiny.

"I don't *know*," says Ralphie. "All I did was pick up her pen during the spelling test today. That's what I get for being nice."

"MWAH! MWAH! MWAH!" Sid Chitterer makes big, wet kissing noises.

Ralphie tries covering his ears. He tries shutting his eyes. Nothing seems to help. It seems as if everyone in the lunchroom is laughing and pointing at him.

"I hate Mondays," Ralphie says.

"Don't let it get to you," Louie says. "Remember, we have an arcade to build after school. Stay focused!"

"Easy for you to say," Ralphie says.

4

BONES

I don't like this game," Tiny says. "Maybe you should find someone else."

"You're perfect for it. Who else are we going to get to be the mouse for whack-a-mouse?"

"I could do it," Chad says.

"We'd need bigger holes," Ralphie

points out. "And a different name."

Louie makes notes on his clipboard. "I'll work on it. Tiny, we can move you to the rope climb."

"But I'm afraid of heights," Tiny says.

Louie sighs. "You can give out the tickets. Are you afraid of tickets?"

"Not usually," says Tiny.

"What about me?" asks Fluffy.

"I have something special in mind for you," Louie says. He brings Fluffy over to a refrigerator box with a big hole cut in it. "You're going to be a fortune-teller!"

"But . . . I don't know how to tell fortunes," Fluffy admits.

"It doesn't matter. You just make stuff up," Louie says. "We're going to call you . . . *Madame Rabbitski!*"

"Ooh, that sounds mysterious. I like it!" Fluffy says.

"We need more room for the ring-toss," Ralphie notes. "If we spread out any more, we'll end up in the Haunted House's yard."

"Maybe one of us should ask the owner if we can use the yard," Fluffy suggests.

"Sounds like a job for our *supervisor,*" Chad says.

Everyone looks at Louie. Louie forces himself to look over at the Haunted House. It *would* give them more room if they could use its yard. But that would mean he'd have to go up and ring the doorbell.

Louie swallows hard. He takes a few steps toward the front door. But the closer he gets, the more he thinks he hears noises.

Rattle, rattle . . . clatter, clatter . . .

Maybe it's bones, Louie thinks. *The bones of other kids who made the mistake of ringing the doorbell.*

Louie makes a big show of looking up at the sky and checking his watch.

"Let's call it a day, team," he says. "It's getting dark—and we don't want Chad to be late for dinner."

5

WHO'S THE BOSS?

Louie and Ralphie's father, Big Lou, has made his specialty for dinner—spaghetti and meatballs.

"So . . . what's new at school, boys?" Big Lou asks. He makes sure to give everyone's meatballs a generous sprinkle of Parmesan cheese.

"Ralphie has a girlfriend," says Louie.

Ralphie groans. "I do NOT," he says.

"There's nothing wrong with liking a girl," Big Lou says. "Your mama was a girl. When I first met her I was just about your age, Ralphie."

The Ratsos take a moment to think about Mama Ratso. Even though she's gone, she's always in their hearts.

"Well, I don't like *this* girl. At ALL," says Ralphie. "Her name is Stinky

Stanko, and she STINKS. For some

reason, everyone at school is saying

I like her. Which I DON'T. Except for handing her a pen today, I've never even gone near her."

"No one has," says Louie.

"Then how do you know she stinks?" Big Lou asks.

"There are some things you just *know,*" Ralphie says.

"Like that the house next to our arcade is haunted," Louie blurts. Just saying the word *haunted* gives him the creeps.

"Haunted?" Big Lou grunts. "Someone's living there. At least, they used to, years ago. Wonder what happened to them?"

"Maybe the *ghost* got them," Ralphie suggests.

"HA!" Big Lou laughs. "There's no such thing as ghosts," he says. "I've never seen one. Have you?"

Ralphie shakes his head and laughs, too. "I'm not afraid of anything," he says.

"Really? I'm afraid of lots of things," Big Lou admits.

"You are?" says Louie.

"Sure," Big Lou says. "Spiders, for one. They give me the creeps."

Louie and Ralphie shudder. Spiders *are* creepy.

"I just tell myself it's OK to be afraid," says Big Lou. "And I try to be brave."

"How?" asks Louie.

"By reminding myself that *I'm* the boss of me, not my fears," Big Lou explains.

"I might be afraid of two things," Ralphie admits. "Stinky Stanko, and people thinking I like her."

"Maybe you both need to tell your fears who's boss," says Big Lou.

"Maybe I need to have another meatball," says Ralphie, holding out his plate. "With extra sprinkly cheese."

Louie tries to focus on his dinner, but with such a lump in his throat, he can't eat. How can he tell a *ghost* he's the boss?

6

THE WRITING ON THE WALL

Tiny Crawley corners Ralphie as soon as he arrives at school.

"Is it true?" he asks.

"Is what true?" asks Ralphie.

"That you walked Stinky Stanko home from school yesterday?" Tiny says. "And that you were *holding her hand*?"

Ralphie drops his schoolbag. He stands on the front steps of the school. "ATTENTION, EVERYONE!" he shouts.

"I DO NOT LIKE STINKY STANKO.

I REPEAT: *I DO NOT LIKE STINKY STANKO!*"

"Then why were you walking her home and holding her hand yesterday?" Sid Chitterer says.

"I wasn't! I wasn't!" Ralphie insists.

It's no use. Everyone is already laughing.

"This stinks. In more ways than one," says Ralphie.

"The more you deny it, the worse it's going to get," says Louie.

"But what else can I do?" Ralphie asks.

Louie stops to think. "Well, someone has to be starting these rumors. Maybe you need to find out who it is."

"I know exactly where to start," says Ralphie. He marches over to Kurt Musky.

"What's up, lover boy?" says Kurt.

"Who's the one who's been telling you about me and Stinky?" asks Ralphie.

"I heard it from Sid," says Kurt.

Sid Chitterer tells Ralphie he heard it from his brother, Mitt. Mitt heard it from Velma Diggs.

"I didn't hear it from anyone," Velma says. "I saw it written on the wall in the girls' room."

"I've hit a wall. Literally," Ralphie tells his friends at lunch. "How can I find out who started the rumor now?"

"Maybe we need to see what's written on the wall," says Louie.

"But it's in the *girls' room*," Tiny reminds them. "That's off-limits to us."

"Not to all of us," says Louie.

Everyone at the table gets quiet. Fluffy looks up from her pickled-beet-and-eggplant sandwich.

"What?" she says. "Why are you all looking at me?"

"You're needed for an important mission," Ralphie says.

After lunch, the Ratso brothers wait outside the girls' room while Fluffy goes inside. She comes out a few minutes later, shaking her head.

"It says 'Ralphie Ratso likes Stinky Stanko,' and then it says 'R.R. walked S.S. home from school yesterday and held her hand.'"

"Go back in there and get rid of it!" Ralphie shouts, pushing Fluffy toward the door.

"I tried already," says Fluffy. "It's written in purple ink that doesn't wash off."

"Written in *purple?*" says Ralphie. He smacks his forehead. "I'll be right back."

Ralphie goes back into the lunch-room. Everyone else has already gone back to class. Except for Stinky Stanko.

"Why did you start those rumors about me?" he asks her.

"How did you know?" she asks.

"The purple ink on the girls' room wall. It came from your purple pen, didn't it?" Ralphie says.

Stinky sighs. "Everyone likes you," she says. "I figured if people thought you liked me, then they'd like me, too. No one has wanted to be friends with me since people started calling me 'Stinky,' which made everyone assume that I stink. So I thought I'd start my own rumor."

Ralphie blinks.

"I'm really sorry," Stinky says. She starts to cry. "Are you going to tell everyone it was me?"

Ralphie isn't thinking about telling anyone. He's remembering who started the rumor about Stinky. It was *him,* back when he and Louie were trying to act tough all the time. He was joking around with Kurt and Sid when he made up the nickname "Stinky Stanko." At the time, it just sounded really funny. But it doesn't seem funny at all now.

"I think I'm the one who's sorry," Ralphie says.

7

DING!
CRASH!

Earth to Ralphie," Chad says. "Are you going to try to whack me, or what?"

Unlike Chad, Ralphie can't seem to keep his head in the game. He keeps thinking about Stinky, and about the look on her face when he told her he was the one who first came up with her terrible nickname. She'd been crying, but when he told her, she'd stopped. She had looked him in the eye and said, "The one who really stinks is YOU, Ralphie Ratso!"

Ralphie has never felt more rotten in his life. What feels even worse is knowing he deserves to feel this way.

"Madame Rabbitski sees . . . a headache in Chad's future," Fluffy says. Even though her "crystal ball" is just a spray-painted fishbowl, she's getting pretty good at fortune-telling.

"This mallet is bigger than me. How will I ever ring the bell?" Tiny says.

"Just hit it as hard as you can," Louie says. "We need to make sure all these games work before the big opening."

"OK, here goes nothing," Tiny says.

He swings the mallet. When it comes
down, the bell rings.

DING!

And then it goes flying.

CRASH! goes a window in the Haunted House.

"Uh-oh," Tiny says.

"Madame Rabbitski sees . . . a tough break in Tiny's future," Fluffy says.

"In everyone's future," Chad says. "That bell was the only thing here that wasn't made of junk. We don't have any money to buy another one."

"That was our best game, too," says Ralphie.

"Not so fast," Louie says. He looks up at the house. The broken window looks like a glaring eye.

"Are you really going to go get it?" Ralphie asks.

Louie doesn't answer. He is already walking up to the house. *It's OK to be afraid,* he tells himself. He takes a deep breath and presses the doorbell.

At first, Louie doesn't hear anything. Maybe the doorbell doesn't work. Or maybe it makes a sound that only the ghosts can hear. As goose bumps prickle up and down Louie's arms, he remembers what Big Lou said.

I'm the boss, I'm the boss, Louie tells himself.

From inside the house, he can hear noises.

Rattle, rattle . . . clatter, clatter . . .

Don't run. Don't run, Louie tells himself. But he couldn't run if he tried; his feet feel like two blocks of cement.

Suddenly, the rattling and clattering stop. The front door opens.

Creeeeeeeeeaaaaaak . . .

And then, Louie sees—

A pair of red eyes staring right at him!

8

NUTS, NUTS, AND MORE NUTS

It really is a ghost! Louie thinks.

He's about to scream, but then he realizes that the pair of red eyes is attached to a face. The face belongs to a little old man. The old man is pale and white—paler and whiter than anyone Louie has ever seen.

"Can I help you?" the old man asks.

Louie stands up straight. He takes a deep breath. "My friends and I were playing a game next door, and our bell went through your window," he explains. "May I please get it back?"

The little old man squints at Louie.

"My eyes aren't so good, so you'll have to find it yourself," he says. "Come on in, sonny boy. My name is Mr. Nutzel, by the way."

"I'm Louie Ratso," Louie says as he follows Mr. Nutzel inside.

Louie can't believe his eyes. No wonder there was so much furniture and junk piled outside the house— the inside is filled with nothing but nuts. Acorns, peanuts, hazelnuts, pecans, and almonds rattle and clatter around Louie as he makes his way through the rooms. *Those must have been the sounds I've been hearing,* he thinks. *It's not ghosts or bones— it's NUTS!*

Louie follows Mr. Nutzel up the stairs. Everywhere he looks, he sees nuts, nuts, and more nuts. "Did you collect all these, sir?" Louie asks.

"I did," says Mr. Nutzel. "I still do. But only at night; the sunlight bothers my eyes."

Louie realizes that the ghost everyone thought they were seeing was probably Mr. Nutzel, gathering at night. All this time, everyone has been afraid of a little old man. Everyone, including Louie.

Up in the attic, on top of a large pile of dusty acorns, is the bell. Louie picks it up and dusts it off. "Thanks, Mr. Nutzel. We're really sorry about your window. We can pay to get it fixed."

"Don't worry about it," the old man says. "Spending some time with you was payment enough. I don't get many visitors these days. It's almost as if people are afraid of me."

"Maybe you could come to the arcade we built," Louie suggests. "We're having our grand opening on Saturday, and everyone is invited."

Mr. Nutzel shakes his head. "I wish I could," he says. "It makes me happy to see that lot so clean, and to know that you kids are enjoying it. But I can't go out in the sun with my eyes the way they are. I can't do much of anything anymore."

Louie looks out the attic window and sees Ralphie and Fluffy and Chad and Tiny down at the arcade, waiting for him. He gives them a wave.

"Well, I should be going," he says. "We need to finish getting ready for the grand opening. It was nice meeting you, Mr. Nutzel."

"You, too, sonny boy," Mr. Nutzel says. "Come back any time."

"Are you OK?" Tiny asks when Louie returns. "We were about to decide which one of us was going to run for help."

"I'm fine. And I got our bell back," Louie says.

"Hooray!" says Fluffy.

"I can't believe you just walked up to the door like that," Ralphie says. "Weren't you afraid of the ghost?"

"I was afraid," Louie admits. "But I told my fear who's boss. It turns out the ghost is just an old man named Mr. Nutzel. He seemed pretty lonely and sad."

"Can he help us get rid of the rest of this junk?" Tiny asks. "We could fit more people if we had more room."

"I don't know if Mr. Nutzel can help us, but I know a way we can help him," Louie says.

Ralphie looks up at his brother. He knows a way he can help someone, too—and be brave like Louie.

- 9 -

RALPHIE TAKES A STAND

I have nothing to say to you, Ralphie Ratso," Stinky says when he approaches her in the lunchroom. She turns away from him and eats her sandwich.

Ralphie looks around the lunchroom and imagines all his friends laughing at him. *I'm afraid,* he thinks. *But I'm also brave.*

"Well, *I* have something to say," Ralphie says. He climbs up on the seat next to Stinky and faces the rest of the lunchroom. He takes a deep breath.

"ATTENTION, EVERYONE!" he shouts. "I WANT YOU ALL TO KNOW THAT I'M NOT CALLING STINKY STANKO 'STINKY' ANYMORE. I'M GOING TO CALL HER BY HER REAL NAME. . . ." Ralphie leans down. "What *is* your real name?" he whispers to Stinky.

"Millicent," she says.

"HER NAME IS MILLICENT," Ralphie continues, "AND SHE IS A NICE PERSON AND SHE DOESN'T SMELL ANY WORSE THAN THE REST OF US. AND IF ANYONE IS MEAN TO HER FROM NOW ON, YOU'RE GOING TO HAVE TO ANSWER TO ME."

After that last part, Ralphie gives the stink eye to Kurt and Sid. They sink down in their seats.

"You didn't have to do that," Millicent says as Ralphie climbs down.

"Actually, I did," he says.

"How can I thank you?" she asks.

"You don't have to," Ralphie says. "But if you want, you can come with me tomorrow. Do you like games?"

BRAVE TOGETHER

I don't know about this," Millicent says.

"It'll be great," says Ralphie.

"But what if your friends don't like me? What if they don't want to be friends with me?" she asks.

"If they're really *my* friends, they'll want to be *your* friend," Ralphie says.

"I'm afraid," Millicent says.

Ralphie takes her hand. "Let's be brave together," he says.

"Is this Millicent?" Tiny asks. "Nice to meet you! I'm Tiny."

"Nice to meet you, too," says Millicent. She shakes his hand, and Louie's, and Fluffy's, and Chad's.

"Wow, you don't stink at all. Actually, you smell kind of nice," says Chad.

"Watch it," says Ralphie, giving him a nudge.

"It's OK," says Millicent. "I do smell nice. I make my own perfume. I call this one *Vanillicent*."

"Mmm," says Fluffy.

"Maybe you could make some perfume for prizes," Louie suggests. "Do you want to work the prize booth?"

"Sure!" says Millicent.

"Let's do this. All this vanilla perfume is making me hungry," says Chad.

"Uh-oh," says Ralphie, reaching for the emergency snacks.

"I'll be right back. I need to do one more thing," says Louie.

Louie runs up the steps of Mr. Nutzel's house and rings the doorbell. A few moments later, he hears rattling and clattering, and the door opens.

"Hello there, sonny boy," Mr. Nutzel says, squinting. "Did you lose your bell again?"

"No," says Louie. "I made you something."

He shows Mr. Nutzel a special chair that Louie has made just for him.

"This way, you can be outside without hurting your eyes. You can watch all the action at the arcade," Louie explains.

"That's very kind of you," says Mr. Nutzel. "But I don't know . . . I haven't been out in a while. . . ."

"It's OK to be afraid," Louie says. "Being brave is hard. Believe me, I know."

"Ready for the grand opening, kids?" Big Lou says.

"Dad!" shouts Ralphie. "You came!"

"I did, and I brought my truck, so I can take all this junk to the dump," Big Lou says. "And my tools, so I can fix Mr. Nutzel's window."

"What's in the cooler?" asks Louie.

"Lemonade, popcorn, and oatmeal walnut cookies," Big Lou says. "You can't have an arcade without a refreshment stand."

"Mmm," says Chad. *"Refreshments."*

"Did you say . . . oatmeal *walnut* cookies?" Mr. Nutzel asks Big Lou.

"Madame Rabbitski sees . . . a future filled with sweet rewards," Fluffy says.

"Ladies and gentlemen, boys
and girls!" Louie shouts.

"The Big City FunTime Arcade

is open for business!"

BOOK THREE

THE INFAMOUS RATSOS

Project Fluffy

For Scott, who is the dreamiest
K. L.

For Darrell, my lifelong and true friend
M. M.

1

EVERYONE LOVES CHUCK

ATTENTION, STUDENTS!" Principal Otteriguez announces to the lunchroom. "In honor of Poetry Month, Peter Rabbit Elementary will be holding its first annual poetry contest!"

"Poetry?" says Chad Badgerton.

"*Bo*-ring," says Ralphie.

"Shh," says Louie. "I can't hear what he's saying."

"First, second, and third prize will be gift certificates to Clawmart!" Mr. Otteriguez announces. "The contest ends on Thursday after school, and we'll reveal the winners next Friday!"

"Poetry is so . . . sappy," says Chad.

"Not all of it. Miss Beavers has been showing us some really funny poems," says Tiny.

"Mr. Ferretti says that poetry is about *feelings*," says Chad. "*Blech.*"

"All art is about feelings," Millicent informs him.

"And about connecting through feelings," Tiny adds. "Love, anger, joy, sadness . . ."

"Like I said," says Chad. *"Blech."*

"Well, I'm going to use *my* feelings to win that contest. In fact, I already have a plan," Louie says. He looks at Ralphie. "We'll write a poem together, and then we'll use the first-prize Clawmart gift certificate to buy ourselves skateboards!"

"Oh, boy! We've been talking about getting skateboards forever," says Ralphie. "No more walking to school. We can ride in style!"

"Are you gonna eat that?" Chad asks, pointing at Tiny's brownie.

"Go for it," says Tiny.

"I love chocolate," says Chad.

"If you love it so much, why don't you write a poem about it?" asks Ralphie.

"I don't love it *that* much," says Chad through a mouthful of brownie.

"Speaking of love..." says Millicent.

She looks over at Chuck Wood in the hot lunch line and bats her eyelashes. "Isn't he *dreamy*?"

"I wish I were friends with Chuck," says Tiny. "Everyone does. He's the coolest."

"Don't you think he's dreamy, Fluffy?" Millicent asks.

But Fluffy isn't listening. She's writing in her green notebook. She's been writing in it and looking through a stack of library books all through lunch.

"What are you scribbling in that thing?" Millicent asks. "Are you already working on a poem?"

"No, it's plans for my garden," Fluffy says.

"You have your own garden?" Millicent asks.

"I have my own plot in the community garden, at the Big City Park," Fluffy explains. "I want to make sure I have room for all my favorite fruits and vegetables."

"I do *not* love fruits and vegetables," says Chad.

"You're missing out," says Fluffy. "You can't just eat junk food all day."

"I can try," Chad says, licking brownie crumbs off his fingers.

Fluffy's gardening books fall off the lunch table. Chuck Wood picks them up.

"Thank you," says Fluffy.

"Gardening, huh?" says Chuck. "My grandma likes to garden."

"Gardening is not just for *grandmas*," Fluffy informs him.

"OK," says Chuck. "See you around."

"Oh, isn't he the *sweetest?*" Millicent says, sighing.

Tiny sighs, too. "And the *coolest*," he says.

"I think it would be *cool* if you all gave me your *sweets*," Chad says, helping himself to everyone else's brownies.

2

PROJECT FLUFFY

We only have a week to get our poem together," says Louie as the Ratso brothers walk home from school. "We'd better start right away."

"Righto," says Ralphie. "So, what should we write about?"

"Leave the thinking to me," says Louie. He considers himself the smart one.

"Hey, wait up!" says a voice behind them. It's Chuck Wood. "I thought maybe we could walk together, since I live about a block away from you guys."

"You want to walk with *us*?" says Louie. "I mean, sure. That's cool."

"I heard you're the ones who put together the Big City FunTime Arcade," Chuck says.

"Yep. We're open every Saturday morning," Louie informs him.

"You're great at planning things," says Chuck. "Do you think you could help *me* plan something?"

"Sure," says Louie. "What is it?"

Chuck looks at Ralphie, then at Louie.

"It's . . . kind of secret," he says.

"Chuck and I need to talk for a while," Louie informs his brother. *"Alone."*

"What about our poem?" Ralphie asks.

"We'll work on it later," says Louie.

Ralphie rolls his eyes. He lets them walk ahead.

"OK," says Louie. He takes his clipboard out of his backpack. "So, what's this project?"

"Well . . . it's not really a what. It's a *who*," Chuck says. "There's a girl I like, but I can't seem to get her attention. And you're friends with her."

"You mean Millicent?" Louie says. "Believe me, you have her attention."

"No, I mean the one with the glasses. And those *amazing* ears," says Chuck, sighing.

"Fluffy?" says Louie.

"Fluffy," says Chuck. He smiles. "So, do you think you can help?"

Louie is already making notes on his clipboard.

"Of course. Why don't you sit with us at lunch tomorrow?" he says. "We'll call it Phase One of Project Fluffy."

"Sounds like a plan," says Chuck.

Louie looks up from his clipboard.

"Where's my brother?" he asks.

Ralphie has taken a shortcut home. The Ratso brothers have an after-school routine—they play their favorite video game and eat their favorite snack.

"Want to play *Verminator?*" Ralphie asks when Louie finally gets home.

"I can't," says Louie, making Project Fluffy notes on his clipboard. "I have work to do."

"What about the poetry contest? And the skateboards?" Ralphie asks. But Louie has already gone into their room and closed the door.

Ralphie throws the bag of snacks in the trash. *These Happy Puffs are stale,* he thinks. Or maybe he's just in a not-very-happy mood.

3

SQUEEEEE!

I can't believe Chuck Wood is sitting with us!" Millicent whispers to Tiny.

"Me neither!" Tiny whispers to Millicent. "The coolest of the cool, at *our lunch table!*"

They both make a noise that sounds a lot like "SQUEEEEE!"

"You two need to chill out," says Ralphie. He sees Chad eyeing his pizza and pulls it toward himself.

"I love pizza," says Chad.

"Well, love your own pizza," says Ralphie. "This is mine."

"Start talking," Louie whispers to Chuck, giving him a nudge.

"About what?" Chuck asks.

"Let Fluffy know how cool you are," Louie says.

Chuck clears his throat. "Uh, I think I've seen you in the park before," he says to Fluffy.

"Hmm?" Fluffy says. She doesn't look up. She has her nose in her gardening notebook again.

"Usually I'm playing baseball with my team, the Big City Critters. I'm a really good pitcher," Chuck says. "You should come and watch sometime. We practice every day after school, and we have games on Saturday afternoons."

"Hmm," Fluffy says again, making some notes.

"I love baseball," Tiny says.

"Can we come and watch?" asks Millicent.

"Um, sure," says Chuck. "How about you, Fluffy?"

"What?" she asks.

"Do you want to watch me play baseball in the park?" Chuck asks.

"I don't go to the park to watch baseball," Fluffy informs him. "I go there to garden."

And then she goes back to her notebook.

Chuck looks at Louie. Louie shrugs.

"I guess it's time for Phase Two," he says.

"What's Phase Two?" asks Chuck.

"Come to my place after school," says Louie.

"Just what I need," grumbles Ralphie. "More of the Louie and Chuck Show."

"I know what *I* need," Chad says, wiggling his eyebrows.

Ralphie sighs and pushes his tray of pizza across the table.

– 4 –

WITH LOVE, CHUCKY

So, what's Phase Two?" Chuck asks back at the Ratsos' apartment.

"Forget Phase Two, when are we going to work on our poem for the contest?" Ralphie asks his brother.

"First things first," says Louie, taking out his clipboard.

"Ugh, I just can't win," Ralphie says. He turns on his video game. "Except when I'm playing *Verminator*."

"Speaking of poems," Louie says to Chuck, "I think you should write one for Fluffy!"

"Um, I'm not really a writer," he says.

"That's OK," Louie says. "You just tell me what you want to say, and I'll do the rest."

"What I want to say? To Fluffy?" says Chuck. "I want her to like me. Everyone likes me."

"Not everyone," mumbles Ralphie.

"She should know I'm cool, and I'm fun, and I'm really good at sports," adds Chuck.

"OK, great," says Louie. He scribbles, then crosses things out.

Then he scribbles some more. Then he crumples up the paper and starts again. And again. And again.

"This is taking forever," Chuck says.

"No one said writing poetry was easy," Louie informs him.

Chuck sighs. "That game looks cool," he says to Ralphie. "Can I play?"

"I don't think it would be fair," Ralphie says. "I'm the high scorer."

"Don't worry. I'm a quick learner," Chuck says, grabbing a controller. Ralphie sighs and resets the game.

"Prepare to be *verminated*," he says.

"Aha!" Louie says about an hour later. "I think I'm finished!"

"Me, too," says Chuck. He's entering his initials as the new high scorer. "*Verminator* was way easier than I thought. Sorry I beat you all those times, Ralphie."

"Not as sorry as I am," Ralphie grumbles, shoving away the controller.

Louie stands up. "Get a load of this," he says.

Dear Fluffy,

Don't you know how **Sporty** I am,
how <u>cool</u> I am,
how <u>popular</u> in <u>school</u> <u>I</u> am?
Won't you give me a glance?
If we found romance.....
. ... you would be <u>so</u> lucky.
    — with love, Chucky.

"Not bad," Chuck says. "But my name is Chuck, not Chucky."

"It's called *poetic license,*" Louie informs him. "Don't worry, Fluffy

will love it. Girls love mushy poetry.
It's, like, a fact."

"She'd better," Chuck says. "I can't take much more of this romance stuff."

"Me neither," Ralphie grumbles.

- 5 -
OOPS

The next day is Saturday. After Louie works at the arcade with his friends, he meets Chuck at the park.

"OK, here's the poem. I copied it on my dad's good paper, and I made sure to make the handwriting extra messy, like yours," Louie says.

"I hope this won't take long," Chuck says. "My game starts in a few minutes."

"Fancy meeting you here!" says Millicent. "We came to watch you."

"And cheer you on!" says Tiny.

"There's something he has to do first," says Louie. He points Chuck in the direction of the community garden.

"Why is he going over there?" Millicent asks.

"Romance is about to bloom," Louie says. He rubs his hands together.

"Hi, Fluffy," says Chuck.

"Oh, hi . . ." says Fluffy.

"Chuck. My name is Chuck," he says.

"Hmm," Fluffy says. "I don't think these strawberries are ripe yet. Do you?"

"How should I know?" Chuck says. "Look, I made you something."

"I'm kind of busy right now," says Fluffy.

"But my game is starting any minute," Chuck informs her. He waves the paper. "I need you to look at it *now*."

"OK, fine," Fluffy says.

She takes the poem from Chuck.

But she forgets to take off her gardening gloves. What was once a poem is now a muddy, unreadable mess.

"Oops," Fluffy says.

"Hey!" says Chuck. "Louie—I mean, *I* worked hard on that!"

"I'm sorry. What did it say?" Fluffy asks.

Chuck tries to remember. "Uh . . . it was about how cool I am," he says. "A lot of the words even rhymed."

"That's . . . nice," Fluffy says. She goes back to considering her strawberries.

"Hey, is the game gonna start soon?" Millicent asks.

"I hope so. This sign is *heavy*," says Tiny.

"Clearly, Project Fluffy needs to kick things up a notch for Phase Three," Louie decides. "Game ON."

6

LOVE STINKS

Phase Three starts on Monday.

"Jeez, this bouquet was expensive," Chuck says.

"Don't worry. It'll be worth it," says Louie. "Girls love flowers. It's, like, a fact."

But when they get to the lunch table with the bouquet, Fluffy wrinkles her nose.

"*ACHOO! ACHOO!* Can you get those flowers away from me? I'm allergic," Fluffy says, sniffling. "That's why my garden is strictly fruits and vegetables."

Chuck looks at Louie. Louie shrugs.

"I guess I can give these to my mom," Chuck says. "I did forget her birthday last week."

Chad takes a bite of his ice-cream sandwich.

"It's not a gift if you can't eat it," he says.

"Hmm . . . that gives me an idea," says Louie.

Phase Four starts on Tuesday.

"And I thought flowers were pricey," says Chuck.

"You didn't have to get so much candy," says Louie, peering into the bag. "It looks like you bought the whole store."

"Well, I don't know what Fluffy likes, so I just bought what I like," Chuck says. "And I like a *lot* of candy."

"She'll be sweet on you in no time," says Louie. "Girls love candy. It's, like, a fact."

"Did I hear that you boys brought candy to school? You know that's against the rules," says Mr. Ferretti, their teacher. "I'm going to have to confiscate that bag, Mr. Wood."

"Great," Chuck says. "There goes all my savings for a new baseball glove."

"Don't worry," Louie says. "My next idea won't cost a thing."

Phase Five starts on Wednesday.

"You need to show her how strong you are," Louie says. "Girls like strong guys."

"Let me guess," Chad says. "Is it, like, a fact?"

"You're catching on," says Louie.

Chuck sighs and rolls up his sleeves.

"Do you ladies need HELP?" he asks the cafeteria workers, a little too loudly. "I'd be glad to TAKE OUT THE TRASH."

"That's kind of you, Chuck," says Mrs. Weasler.

Chuck lifts the trash bags over his head. He looks in Fluffy's direction and grins.

"My hero," says Millicent.

"What a guy," says Tiny.

"What a *show-off*," says Fluffy. She takes a sip from her carrot juice, then goes back to her gardening notebook.

"Well," says Louie, crossing off another plan on his clipboard. "There goes that idea."

"Don't forget—your entries for the poetry contest are due by the end of the school day tomorrow!" Principal Otteriguez announces to the lunchroom.

"*I* haven't forgotten," says Ralphie, giving his brother a look.

"Did you say something?" Louie asks.

"Nothing important," says Ralphie. "*Clearly.*"

"I have an idea," says Tiny. He turns to Millicent. "There's still time for us to enter the poetry contest together. I can write something about how awesome we think Chuck is."

"And I can illustrate it! Genius!" says Millicent. She and Tiny high-five each other. "We'd better get started right away."

"You're going to write a poem about Chuck? You can't tell a *boy* you think he's cool," Chad informs Tiny as he polishes off his second chocolate pudding. "Not if *you're* a boy."

"Why not?" asks Tiny.

"I don't know," says Chad. "You just can't."

"I give you my dessert every day because I think *you're* cool," Tiny informs him.

"You do?" Chad says. He hesitates ... then pats Tiny on the back. "Actually, I think you're pretty cool, too."

"Thanks," says Tiny.

Chad takes another bite of pudding.

"Mmm," says Chad. "Cool, and sweet . . . and *chocolatey*."

"Why do I think we're not talking about me anymore?" Tiny says.

"I like you a lot, Tiny," says Chad. "But I *love* pudding."

On the way home from school, Chuck can barely carry his books.

"My arms are killing me from lugging those trash bags, and now

I smell like garbage," he says. "Love *stinks!*"

"I think that might just be you," says Ralphie, sniffing.

"This is a *private* conversation," Louie reminds his brother.

"Don't worry, I know the drill," he says, glaring at them.

"I have another idea," Louie tells Chuck.

"What phase are we on now? Seven? Eight?" Chuck asks.

"Phase Six," Louie says. "This one will *definitely* work. I just need to turn

the poem I wrote about Fluffy into a
song, and then you can appear under
her window and serenade her!"

"Serenade?" says Chuck.

"Girls love to be serenaded," Louie
informs him. "It's, like, a fact."

"Sneaking around in the dark under someone's window? Sounds more like *trespassing*," says Ralphie.

"He's right," Chuck says, throwing up his hands. "You know, I might stink right now, but your advice is *really* garbage, Louie. See you around."

"Wait! I thought we were friends!" Louie calls. But Chuck has already stormed off.

"Good riddance," says Ralphie.

"You're just jealous because Chuck is cool and he wants to hang out with me and not you," Louie says.

"He's not a real friend," Ralphie says. "He was just using you to get to Fluffy."

"Well, next time I need your two cents, I'll ask for it," says Louie.

"Oh, yeah?" says Ralphie, stomping off. "We'll see about that."

7

THINKING AND SCRIBBLING

Don't forget — entries for the poetry contest are due after school today by five o'clock!" Principal Otteriguez announces at lunch.

"Uh-oh," says Louie. "We'd better start working on our poem."

"We?" says Ralphie. "This time, you're on your own, big brother."

"But I'm fresh out of ideas," Louie says.

"Maybe because you spent the whole week coming up with ideas for *Chuck*," Ralphie reminds him.

Louie tries to think of ideas all afternoon. He's still drawing a blank when the final bell rings.

"I still have until five. Maybe you guys could help me brainstorm?" Louie says after school.

"Poetry? Blech," says Chad.

"Fluffy, can you help?" Louie says.

"I have to go water my plants," she says.

"How about you guys?" Louie asks Millicent and Tiny.

"We have our own poem to finish," says Millicent.

"Plus, we're really mad at you, Louie Ratso," says Tiny.

"Why?" asks Louie. "What did I do?"

"Because of you, Chuck isn't sitting with us at lunch anymore," says Tiny.

"Now we have to admire him from all the way across the cafeteria again!" says Millicent.

"But I can't do all of this by myself!" Louie says.

He stays after school thinking and scribbling, scribbling and thinking. But nothing sounds right.

It's so much harder working alone, he realizes. *And a lot less fun.*

8

TOUGH WEEK

You're late," Big Lou says when Louie finally gets home.

"I was trying to write something in time to enter the poetry contest," Louie says. "But nothing I came up with was good enough."

Ralphie is already finished with his dinner. "May I have some ice cream?" he asks.

"You may," says Big Lou. He turns back to Louie. "Your meatball grinder is cold now. Do you want me to heat it up?"

"No, that's OK," Louie says. The grinder is cold and a little soggy, but he's too hungry to care.

"You look tired," says Big Lou.

"I've been trying to help a kid at school get a girl to notice him," Louie says. "But Project Fluffy has been a disaster."

"Maybe because Fluffy is a *person* and not a project," Ralphie says, taking a bite of rocky road.

"Ralphie is right. Women aren't projects, or objects," Big Lou notes. "When I first met your mom, I really wanted her to like me, so I figured out what she liked."

"She liked to laugh and to sing," says Louie.

"And she liked strawberry ice cream," says Ralphie. "That's my second favorite, after rocky road."

"That's all true. And she also liked bird-watching," says Big Lou.

"She used to wear binoculars," says Ralphie. "And carry around that little notebook."

"That's where she'd write about the birds she saw," says Louie.

Mama and the boys–Big City Park

"On our first date, we went to the Big City Park and watched the birds," says Big Lou.

"You watched birds?" says Ralphie. "*Bo*-ring!"

"I thought it would be, but it was actually kind of interesting," says Big Lou. "And then, of course, I took her out for strawberry ice cream."

"I bet the ice cream sealed the deal," said Ralphie.

"What sealed the deal came after the ice cream," says Big Lou. "That's when I told her how much I liked her."

"You told her you liked her *to her face*?" Ralphie says.

"It felt pretty great to say it, actually," Big Lou says. "I wish I'd told your mom how I felt about her more often. I'm glad I can tell you boys how much I love you every day."

"I love you, too, Dad," says Louie.

"Me, too," says Ralphie. "Every day."

As Louie eats his soggy sandwich, he thinks about Mama Ratso. Talking about her and all the things she liked makes him feel good. It almost seems as if she's there with them, laughing and eating ice cream.

- 9 -
FRIENDS

At the end of the day on Friday, the whole school assembles in the auditorium.

"I'm proud to introduce the winners of the First Annual Peter Rabbit Elementary School Poetry Contest," Mr. Otteriguez announces. "First prize goes to . . . Millicent Stanko and Tiny Crawley, for their illustrated poem, 'Chuck Steals Home'!"

"SQUEEEE!" exclaim Millicent and Tiny as they high-five each other. After Tiny reads his poem, Millicent shows everyone her drawings.

"They really do make a good team," Louie admits.

"And now, second prize," Mr. Otteriguez announces. "Congratulations to Velma Diggs, for her poem, 'The Hole World'!"

"Whoa, that was deep," Chad says when Velma finishes reading.

"And third prize goes to . . . Ralphie Ratso, for his poem, 'Friends'!"

"What?" Louie says.

"Ahem," Ralphie says. Then he starts reading.

Friends
a rhyming poem by R. Ratso

When it comes to the friends of Ralphie Ratso,
here are some things you should know:

TINY is funny, and really nice.
He's one of my favorite mice.

MILLICENT has amazing hair, a cool
attitude, and artistic flair.

You might think all **CHAD** does is eat,
but I know he can also be funny and sweet.

FLUFFY'S favorite is anything green —
She's the best gardener I've ever seen!

LOUIE is my brother. He's super smart.
I really miss him when we're apart.

MY FRIENDS are the best. I love them so.

I'm the luckiest rat I know.

"That's so beautiful," says Tiny.

"Is someone cutting onions in here?" asks Chad, wiping a tear from his eye.

"Wow," Louie says after the assembly ends. "You wrote that poem?"

"I had a lot of free time this week," Ralphie reminds him.

"Most of what I tried to write was pretty bad," Louie admits. "Except for this part." He hands over his clipboard.

Today I am mizerable
and down on my luck

I feel bad I ignored Ralphie
and spent all my time
        with Chuck.

As long as we're together
I never feel stuck.

"All that time I was trying to figure out what Chuck needed to get Fluffy's attention, and I wasn't paying attention to what *you* needed," Louie says. "I'm really sorry."

"I'm sorry I didn't help *you* when you needed it," Ralphie says. "I think I was jealous, but not because Chuck wanted to hang out with you. Because *you* wanted to hang out with *Chuck*."

"Well, it turned out you didn't need anyone's help. You're a really good writer," Louie says.

"But I only won third place," Ralphie says. "The third-place gift certificate isn't enough to buy two skateboards."

"You should just buy one for yourself. You earned it," Louie suggests.

"Nah, it won't be as much fun riding without you," says Ralphie. His eyes brighten. "But you know, *Verminator 2* is coming out soon. Maybe I'll buy it for us, along with a fresh bag of Happy Puffs."

"As long as we're together, I'm happy enough," Louie says.

"As long as we're together and I'm the high scorer again!" says Ralphie.

"Hey, guys," says Chuck Wood. "What's up, Millicent? Hi, Tiny."

"Oh, hey," says Millicent, pretending not to care.

"Whatever," says Tiny.

"I just wanted to thank you for that poem. I'm really nervous about my game tomorrow, so it's nice to know you're thinking of me," he says.

"It was nothing," says Millicent.

"Whatever," Tiny says again.

"I really liked your drawings of me, Millicent," Chuck says. "You made me look like a real baseball star!"

Millicent blushes. "I just draw what I see," she says.

"And Tiny, I loved the sporty details you put in the poem," Chuck says.

"I had a *ball* writing it," Tiny admits.

"You guys really get me," Chuck says. "Maybe I'll see you tomorrow at the game?"

"Definitely," says Millicent.

"Sure!" says Tiny.

"Don't forget to bring your Chuck signs," Chuck says.

As Chuck walks away, Millicent and Tiny look at each other.

"SQUEEEE!" they say.

As he watches the scene unfold between Chuck and Millicent and Tiny, Louie thinks about his conversation with Ralphie, and what Big Lou said at dinner the night before. He thinks about Mama Ratso and her bird-watching notebook . . . which was *a lot* like Fluffy's gardening notebook. Then he gets an idea, too.

"Wait, Chuck," he says. "I just thought of something nice you could do for Fluffy, just like Millicent and Tiny did for you."

Chuck rolls his eyes. "I'm done with Project Fluffy," he says.

"Me, too," says Louie. "I spent all my time trying to find a way for you to get Fluffy's attention, because that's what *you* wanted. But I wasn't thinking about Fluffy at all. When you like someone, you need to pay attention to what *they* want."

"OK," Chuck says, sighing. "I'm listening."

Louie whispers in his ear.

- 10 -

PIZZA, OR . . . SALAD

Finally," Fluffy says.

That Saturday afternoon, her strawberries look perfectly red and ripe. But just as she's about to pick them, she hears a voice.

"Hey," says Chuck.

"Oh. Hi, Chuck," says Fluffy.

"I know you're busy with your garden, but I just wanted to bring you . . . this bouquet," he says. "Since you're allergic to flowers, I thought you could plant these seeds instead."

"Wow!" Fluffy says, smiling. "This is so . . . thoughtful."

"I just wanted you to know I like you," says Chuck. "If you like me, too, maybe sometime we could go out for pizza, or . . . salad?"

"Chuck," says Fluffy, "I think I could like you as a friend. But my heart belongs to my garden."

"OK," says Chuck. "You know, the more I think about it, my heart really belongs to baseball."

"Friends?" asks Fluffy.

"Definitely," says Chuck. "Friends."

They shake paws. Then Fluffy looks over at the baseball field.

"Um, speaking of baseball, isn't your game about to start?" she asks.

"Thanks for reminding me!" Chuck says. He grabs his glove and runs off.

"I didn't know you were all coming to watch the game," Millicent says.

"I bought an extra foam finger, if anyone wants it," says Tiny.

"We're having a picnic," Louie says.

"And maybe watching some birds," says Big Lou.

"I'm just here for the food," Chad explains. "Well, that and the company."

"Leave some room for dessert, gang—I have fresh-picked straw-berries," says Fluffy.

"I'm feeling inspired," says Ralphie. "Ahem. . . ."

"I love picnics, and baseball,
and sunny weather.
But most of all,
I love when we're all together."

"Game ON!" says Louie.

— DISCUSSION QUESTIONS —

1. The Ratso brothers are no good at being bad. Why do their nasty plans always turn into good deeds?

2. Chad Badgerton's head is way too big for Tiny's hat. Why did he take it in *The Infamous Ratsos*? What do bullies really want?

3. What is the difference between being a bully and being tough? Are the Ratso brothers bullies? Why or why not?

4. What are the advantages of being a softie? By the end of the first book, how do you think Big Lou would answer that question? How would his sons answer it?

5. In *The Infamous Ratsos Are Not Afraid*, Ralphie started a rumor about Millicent and thought it was funny, but then his classmates start teasing *him!* What does it make him realize about what he did to Millicent?

6. Appearances are often not what they seem. How did Louie have to change his thinking about the "ghost" and the haunted house? What did he discover?

7. In *The Infamous Ratsos: Project Fluffy*, what would Chuck Wood have noticed about Fluffy if he had been paying attention to her and what she liked?

8. What are some of the things that Big Lou, Ralphie, and Louie remember about Mama Ratso? What did she like? What are some things that people you know like?

9. Character traits are words used to describe someone. For example, Louie is helpful and Chuck is athletic. What character traits would you use to describe Ralphie? Big Lou? Fluffy? Chad? What character traits would you want your friends to recognize in you?

10. Why does Big Lou think it is so important to tell the people you love how you feel about them? Why does he make sure to tell his boys every day that he loves them?

Kara LaReau is the author of many books for children, including The Infamous Ratsos series and the ZomBert trilogy. About her high-spirited characters, she says, "My grandfather was named Ralph and his older brother was named Louie. Evidently, they were troublemakers back in the day, though the exact nature of their exploits has never been revealed. The Ratsos are what I imagine they were like— trying to seem tough, despite their hearts of gold." Kara LaReau lives in Providence, Rhode Island, with her family.

Matt Myers is the illustrator of
*E-I-E-I-O: How Old MacDonald Got His
Farm (with a Little Help from a Hen)*
by Judy Sierra; *Pirate's Perfect Pet* by
Beth Ferry; and all the books in the
Infamous Ratsos series, as well as many
other books for young readers. About
developing the characters, he says, "My
childhood partner in mischief was Bruce.
I drew Ralphie with Bruce's big black
glasses, minus the tape he needed to mend
them each time our adventures got a little
too crazy." Matt Myers lives in Charlotte,
North Carolina.

Whether it's doing good deeds
for neighbors, learning it's OK to
ask for help, or creating friendships,
the Infamous Ratso brothers are
always discovering new things
in the neighborhood!

A THEODOR SEUSS GEISEL
HONOR BOOK

Available in hardcover and
paperback and as an e-book

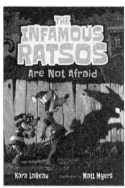

Available in hardcover and
paperback and as an e-book

Available in hardcover and
paperback and as an e-book

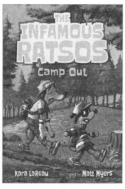

Available in hardcover and
paperback and as an e-book

Available in hardcover and
as an e-book

www.candlewick.com